"Everyone thought I'd be good
at swimming, but I was scared."

Hana

Ernie

MRS WINGER

BETTY

Owen

Francis

Douglas

Hetty

DOUGLAS, THE DUCK WHO WANTED TO SWIM
A RED FOX BOOK 978 1 862 30532 8

First published in Great Britain by Red Fox,
an imprint of Random House Children's Books
A Random House Group Company

This edition published 2008

1 3 5 7 9 10 8 6 4 2

Text © Red Fox 2008
Hana's Helpline © 2006 Calon Limited
Hana's Helpline is a registered trademark of Calon.

Red Fox Books are published by Random House Children's Books,
61–63 Uxbridge Road, London W5 5SA

www.kidsatrandomhouse.co.uk
www.rbooks.co.uk

Addresses for companies within The Random House Group Limited can be found at: www.randomhouse.co.uk/offices.htm

THE RANDOM HOUSE GROUP Limited Reg. No. 954009

A CIP catalogue record for this book is available from the British Library.

Printed in China

DOUGLAS

THE DUCK WHO WANTED TO SWIM

It was time for a swimming lesson. All the other animals were excited, but Douglas didn't like the look of the big swimming pool.

Mrs Winger, the swimming teacher, said, "Come along, Douglas, there's nothing to be afraid of. You'll take to it like a duck to water."

Douglas shook his head sadly; he wanted to jump in but he just couldn't.

Ernie called out, "He's quackers. Douglas is scared of swimming! Douglas is scared of swimming!" Mrs Winger was very cross. "That's quite enough, Ernie," she said.

Douglas stood by the pool edge. He really wanted to get in the water but he couldn't make that first jump.

He looked down, he couldn't get in there! He ran to the corner of the pool.

"Come on, Douglas," called Francis. "Jump in and I'll race you across the pool."

"No!" said Douglas. "I can't do it." And he ran off into the changing room.

"Oh dear," sighed Mrs Winger.

As they walked home, Douglas said to Francis, "Ernie's right.
I am scared of swimming. Mum and Dad will be really upset,
especially Mum. She really wants me to learn to swim."
    "Isn't that your mum there?" said Francis, pointing at
someone in the duck pond.

Douglas's mum was very upset and all wet. Francis and Douglas ran to help. "Mum, it's fine. The pond is shallow. Look," said Douglas.

  "Ooo, I am silly, frightened of a little bit of water," said Douglas's mum.

At home Douglas watched TV and thought about his swimming lesson tomorrow. He was really scared. Just then an advert came on. It was Hana, Francis's mum.

"Whatever your problem, big or small, I'm here to help, so give me a call. Ring Hana's Helpline on Moo, Baa, Double Quack, Double Quack."

To help Douglas feel less scared of swimming, Hana decided
to take it slowly. First Douglas stood in a washing-up bowl full
of water.

"I feel stupid, but I don't feel scared," he said.

"You're doing very well, Douglas," said Hana.

The second stage was the paddling pool. Francis decided to join in, too. Soon Douglas and Francis were having lots of fun. They were so busy that Douglas forgot he was scared of swimming!

Hana said to Owen and Betty, "He seems to be getting on all right now. I think we might be ready for the next stage."

The next stage was the pond in the park. Hana looked at Douglas. "It's just like the paddling pool, Douglas, just a little bit bigger."

Douglas still looked worried. "But Mum was scared when she fell in."
Hana looked confused.
"Your mum fell in this pond?"
Francis piped up, "Douglas's mum is a chicken, you see."
Douglas said, "And she's very scared of water but she doesn't want me to be scared."
"Come on then," said Francis. "Let's get quacking!"

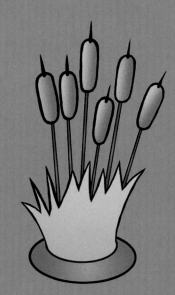

They all jumped in the pond. "Hang on one minute," said
Owen and he pointed at a sign: NO PADDLING.
  "And here comes the park keeper," he added. "He doesn't
look happy."

Finally it was time to try the swimming pool. Hana looked at Douglas. "You see it's harder for birds like your mum and Owen to swim."

  "Because they don't have special swimming feathers like Francis and me," said Douglas.

  "That's right, poppet," said Hana "Now, shall we give it a go?"

Douglas nodded nervously, but as he walked towards the pool, he panicked and tore his rubber ring off. It hit Owen and he fell into the pool.

"HELP, HELP! I can't swim," cried Owen.

"Come on, Douglas," shouted Francis. "Help!"

Douglas froze for a moment and then snapped into action. He jumped into the water with his rings and swam towards Owen.

"Owen, quick, hold onto our rings," said Francis.

Hana and Betty were waiting to help Owen out.

"Look, Mum, I'm swimming," said Douglas.

"I know, I'm so proud of you," said Douglas's mum.

Douglas's mum was scared of water, but in the paddling pool she had fun splashing Francis and Douglas.

"I never knew water could be such fun," she said.

"It's all thanks to you, Hana, and to Francis," said Douglas.

Hana smiled and put her wings around Betty and Owen's shoulders. "I've got a good team to help me," she said.

Hana's Help Point

Hana's Tips for a Happy Worry-Free Swimming Time

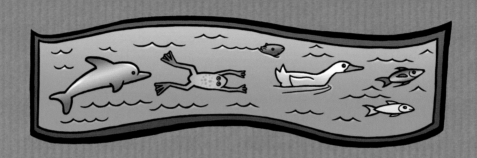

If you feel frightened and don't like going near water, don't worry! Hana can help!

Take things slowly

★ ALWAYS make sure an adult is looking after you.

★ Don't try to rush into anything.

★ Get used to being in the water gradually.

★ Try paddling in a paddling pool or a bath.

Pool Rules

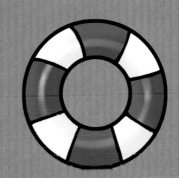

★ Be safe around the water.

★ Don't run.

★ Be careful about jumping in.

★ Don't go too close to the edge of the pool.

Pool Fun

★ Life vests are good for when you first start to swim.

★ Armbands can be a big help, too.

★ Floats and rubber rings are fun to use in the pool.

★ Goggles will help you see under the water.

★ A rubber duck is good for the bath!

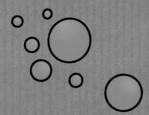

DON'T FORGET YOUR TOWEL!!

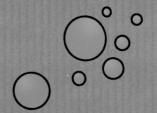

"So remember . . .

. . . if you're in trouble and you need help, ring me, Hana, on **Moo, Baa, Double Quack, Double Quack!**"